THREE
UP A TREE

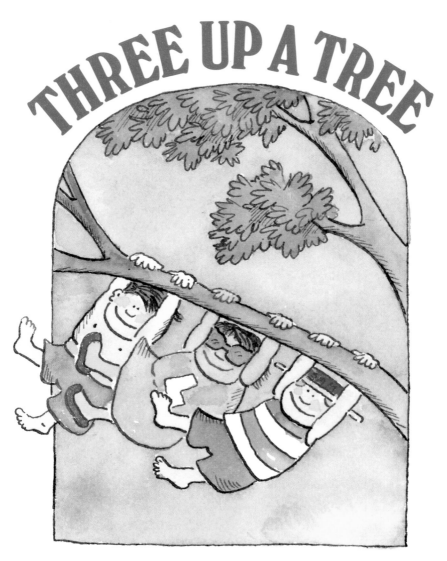

THREE UP A TREE

by James Marshall

Dial Books for Young Readers / New York

Dial easy-to-read

Published by Dial Books for Young Readers
A Division of NAL Penguin Inc.
2 Park Avenue
New York, New York 10016

Published simultaneously in Canada by
Fitzhenry & Whiteside Limited, Toronto
Copyright © 1986 by James Marshall
Printed in Hong Kong by South China Printing Co.
The Dial Easy-to-Read logo is a registered trademark of
Dial Books for Young Readers,
a division of NAL Penguin Inc., ®TM 1,162,178.

Library of Congress Cataloging in Publication Data
Marshall, James, 1942– Three up a tree.
Summary: Sam and Spider build a tree house and
go there with Lolly to trade stories.
[1. Storytelling—Fiction.
2. Tree Houses—Fiction.] I. Title.
PZ7.M35672Th 1986 [E] 86-2163
(b)

First Hardcover Printing 1986
ISBN 0-8037-0328-7 (tr.)
ISBN 0-8037-0329-5 (lib. bdg.)
5 7 9 10 8 6 4

First Trade Paperback Printing 1989
ISBN 0-8037-0596-4 (ppr.)
3 5 7 9 10 8 6 4 2

The art for each picture consists of an ink and
watercolor painting, which is camera-separated
and reproduced in full color.

Reading Level 1.8

For Toby Sherry

"Wow!" said Spider.

"Will you look at *that*!"

Some big kids down the street

had built a swell tree house.

"Can we come up?" called out Sam.

"No!" said the big kids.

"Well!" said Spider.

"Never mind," said Sam.

"We'll build our own tree house."

"Let's ask Lolly to help,"

said Spider.

But Lolly would not help.

"I'm too busy," she said.

"You call *that* busy?" said Spider.

"Let's go," said Sam.

In no time Spider and Sam

were as busy as squirrels.

Meanwhile Lolly decided

to take a little snooze.

When Lolly woke up

the tree house was finished.

"Wow," she said.

"I'll be right up."

"Oh, no," said Sam.

"You didn't help."

"Oh, *please*," said Lolly.

"No!" said Spider.

"I know some good stories,"

said Lolly.

"Stories?" said Sam.

"I love a good story."

Lolly was up the tree in a flash.

"Now tell us a story," said Sam.

"And make it good," said Spider.

"Sit down," said Lolly.

"And listen to this."

12

Lolly's Story

One summer evening

a doll and a chicken

went for a walk.

And they got lost.

"Oh, no," said the doll.

Just then a monster

came around the corner.

"Oh, no," said the doll.

"Let's run!"

cried the chicken.

And they ran as fast

as they could.

"He's right behind us!"

cried the chicken.

"Oh, no!"

said the doll.

"Quick!" cried the chicken.

"Let's climb that tree!"

And they did—

in a jiffy.

But monsters know how

to climb trees too.

"He's got us now!" cried the chicken.

"Oh, no!" cried the doll.

The monster opened his mouth.

"Will you tie my new shoes?"

he said.

"Oh, yes!" said the doll.

19

"Not much of a story,"
said Spider.

"The end was too sweet."

"Can you tell a better story?"
said Lolly.

"Listen to this," said Spider.

Spider's Story

A chicken caught the wrong bus.
She found herself
in a bad part of town—
the part of town where foxes live.
"Uh-oh," she said.

Quickly she pulled down her hat
and waited for the next bus.
But very soon—you guessed it—
a hungry fox came along
and sat beside her.

His eyes were not good.

But there was nothing wrong

with his nose.

"I can smell that you're having

chicken tonight," he said.

"Er..." said the chicken.

"Yes, I have just been to the store."

"I *love* chicken,"

said the fox.

"How will you cook it?"

The chicken knew

she had to be clever.

She did not want the fox

to invite himself to dinner.

"Well," she said.

"I always cook my chicken

in sour chocolate milk

with lots of pickles and rotten eggs."

"It sounds delicious,"

said the fox.

"May I come to dinner?"

"Let's see," said the chicken.

"That will make ten of us."

Well, *that* was too many

for the fox!

He grabbed the chicken's grocery bag

and ran away.

"All for me!" he cried.

"All for me!"

The poor chicken flew up
into a nearby tree
to wait for the next bus.
(She should have done that
in the first place.)

P.S. When the fox got home,
he reached into the bag.
But there was no chicken inside.
Only the chicken's favorite food.
Can you guess what it was?

"Worms!" cried Lolly. "Worms!
That story wasn't bad."

"Not bad at all," said Sam.

"But now it's *my* turn."

Sam's Story

A monster woke up from a nap.

He was *very* hungry.

"I want ice cream," he said.

"Lots of it."

He went out to buy some.

But he got lost.

"Oh, well," he said.

"I'll just ask someone for help."

At that moment a fox

came around the corner.

"Excuse me," said the monster.

"Help!" cried the fox.

"I'm getting out of here!"

And away he went.

"How rude," said the monster.

He put on the fox's hat,
scarf, and glasses.

Just then a doll and a chicken
came around the corner.

"Hi," said the chicken.

"Will you help me find
some ice cream?" said the monster.
"If you will give us a ride
in your wagon," said the chicken.
And off they went.

"Stop!" said the chicken.

"This is the place for ice cream."

"Oh really?" said the monster.

"Wait here," said the doll.

"We'll be right back."

In a moment they were back.

"Step on it!" said the doll.

"You don't want your ice cream
to melt!"

"I'll hurry!" said the monster.

"Faster!" cried the chicken.

The monster ran as fast as he could.

Soon they came to a big tree.

"This is where we live,"

said the doll.

And they all climbed up the tree.

The doll and the chicken

opened their bags.

But there was

no ice cream inside.

There was only money.

"Oh, no!" said the monster.

"You are bank robbers!"

The monster took off his hat,

scarf, and glasses.

The doll and the chicken

were scared out of their wits.

"Help, help!" they cried.

"Let's get out of here!"

And they ran as fast as their

little legs could carry them.

The monster returned
the money to the bank.
As a reward he was given
all the ice cream he could eat.
And there was *lots* of it!

"My story was better," said Lolly.

"No, mine was," said Spider.

"No, mine!" said Sam.

"Let's hear them again," said Lolly.

And they did.